I Found Myself . . .

The Last Dreams

I Found Myself . . .
  The Last Dreams

NAGUIB MAHFOUZ

translated and with an introduction by Hisham Matar
and photographs by Diana Matar

PENGUIN
VIKING

VIKING

UK | USA | Canada | Ireland | Australia
India | New Zealand | South Africa

Viking is part of the Penguin Random House group of companies
whose addresses can be found at global.penguinrandomhouse.com.

Penguin Random House UK,
One Embassy Gardens, 8 Viaduct Gardens, London SW11 7BW

penguin.co.uk

Published by arrangement with Omkalthoum Mahfouz
First published as a New Directions Paperbook (NDP 16xx) 2025
First published in Great Britain by Viking 2025

001

Copyright © the Estate of Naguib Mahfouz
Translation and afterword copyright © Hisham Matar, 2025
Photographs copyright © Diana Matar, 2025

The moral right of the author has been asserted

Penguin Random House values and supports copyright.
Copyright fuels creativity, encourages diverse voices, promotes freedom
of expression and supports a vibrant culture. Thank you for purchasing
an authorized edition of this book and for respecting intellectual property
laws by not reproducing, scanning or distributing any part of it by any
means without permission. You are supporting authors and enabling
Penguin Random House to continue to publish books for everyone.
No part of this book may be used or reproduced in any manner for the
purpose of training artificial intelligence technologies or systems. In accordance
with Article 4(3) of the DSM Directive 2019/790, Penguin Random House
expressly reserves this work from the text and data mining exception

Printed and bound in Great Britain by Clays Ltd, Elcograf S.p.A.

The authorized representative in the EEA is Penguin Random House Ireland,
Morrison Chambers, 32 Nassau Street, Dublin D02 YH68

A CIP catalogue record for this book is available from the British Library

ISBN: 978-0-241-77413-7

Penguin Random House is committed to a sustainable future
for our business, our readers and our planet. This book is made from
Forest Stewardship Council® certified paper.

Introduction

Naguib Mahfouz was having the dreams in this book around the time when my wife, the photographer Diana Matar, and I met him at a secret location in Cairo. This was in the time after October 15, 1994, the day when, in one of the alleyways he frequented on his daily walk, the author was attacked by a stranger who proceeded to stab him repeatedly in the neck. The story then goes that Mahfouz took himself to hospital and waited his turn, pressing his hand—the same hand with which he had, by this time, written over forty novels, a couple of autobiographical books, and several hundred articles—against the open gash in the side of his neck, telling the nurse, in his characteristically soft voice, at once informal and given to social conviviality, "It's nothing serious," before revealing to her the fountain of blood.

Up to then, Mahfouz's regimen was famously predictable: the cafés where he was a regular, the streets where he passed, where everyone knew him and knew not to interrupt him. Now his movements were prescribed. This was as much due to concerns for his safety as it was to his waning health: old age had been violently advanced by the assault. Now he almost never walked alone in public. He met friends at an undisclosed venue for their weekly soirees. An acquaintance got us an invitation.

The hotel was out of the way and unremarkable, on the

Maadi stretch of the Nile Cornice, facing the water. I was familiar with the place, because once I used to go swimming there and would hand my post to the concierge who had a contact at the local post office, which meant that my mail almost always reached its destination. But all that was years ago. Now my visits to Cairo were brief. The instructions we had were to announce ourselves at reception and say that we were there for the Mahfouz soirée. But the man behind the desk was skeptical.

"Mahfouz? What Mahfouz? And I don't know what you mean by a soirée."

He wrote down our names and went off, asking us to wait there. His colleague sustained a face of affable suspicion. After a few minutes the man returned and now with an entirely changed manner, led us to the elevator. When the doors pulled shut, he blushed a little and said, facing the floor, "Welcome. You have honored us." We got out at the fourteenth floor and followed him to the end of the long corridor. He knocked at the last door, opened it a few inches and announced our names.

The room was a large, cleared-out suite that had been haphazardly furnished with a couple of sofas and armchairs clustered in the middle. The curtains were drawn. Mahfouz, dressed in a dark olive safari suit, stood up and, aided on one side by his assistant and on the other by a wooden crook handle cane, began walking toward us. The ten or so people gathered there also rose. Mahfouz's assistant shouted into his ear, "Mr. Hisham Matar. A Libyan writer. And his American wife, Madam Diana."

Mahfouz hooked his cane on the inside of his elbow and extended both hands to me. His skin was cool and soft. He smiled and asked, whispering his one-word question, "Libyan?"

"Yes," I said, nodding in case I wasn't speaking loudly enough.

"With or against?" he asked slowly.

"Against," I said.

"Excellent," he said. "Come sit beside me."

Much was said that evening, and the comic theme persisted, whereby everyone had to shout while Mahfouz, the only one who was hard of hearing, continued—clearly enjoying the luxury—speaking in a near-whisper, demonstrating the age-old fact that anything, no matter how beautiful or profound, said at a high volume, inevitably sounds empty.

"How many more do I have left?" he suddenly asked his assistant.

"Three," the man yelled.

Mahfouz looked relieved. He lit a cigarette and smoked it with great relish, and each cloud of smoke that left his lungs floated whitely above him. Half an hour later, he asked the same question. "Two," came the answer.

"He is only allowed five a day," the man beside me, a professor of philosophy, explained: "Doctor's orders."

The gathering was made up of writers, critics, and academics. They shouted intelligent questions and bits of literary news. Mahfouz listened modestly, his vein-webbed hands resting on his knees, facing forward, his back not quite touching the sofa, as though careful to take up as little room as possible. It seemed that at any moment he might get up and leave. Every time he was asked a question, there was almost always a gap before he spoke. Waiting for him, we watched him stare ahead. And in response to certain questions, he simply said nothing, held the silence and it stretched until, eventually, someone had the nerve to say something, often attempting to speak for him, which made the silence that followed more weighty than the first.

In response to whether it was true that Stendhal was an important writer for him, he said he had read the Frenchman as a young man and admired his books but that that was so long ago now that he was no longer sure what he would make of Stendhal today.

When asked whether he believed criticism can help a writer, he said, "Of course."

"Would you then say you learned from those who wrote about your work?"

"Of course," he said again.

Then it was my turn to speak, and although I had nothing to say, I leaned closer to him, taking note of his large ear. Anyone looking at us, I thought, would think I was about to confide an intimate detail about my life. But the volume had to be at broadcasting levels.

And no sooner did I ask my question than I regretted it:

"How do you see writers such as myself, Arabs who, having grown up inside another language—in my case the English language—have come to write in it?"

I was young, still in my late twenties, and such questions preoccupied me back then.

His reply came swiftly. "You belong to the language you write in."

A silence stretched.

Then, perhaps to console me, Mahfouz added, "But who cares? Does it matter what language Shakespeare wrote in?"

But, I thought to myself, as the eyes of all those around me waited for me to respond, it matters very much.

Whenever I have told this story, and I have perhaps told it a dozen or two dozen times in the quarter of a century since, I often caught myself adding, for reasons I am yet to fully understand, words that Mahfouz did not speak, words that I have never heard anyone except myself speak, attributing them to him, perhaps using Mahfouz as a cover to add poignancy to what I have always secretly believed and which, that day sitting beside him in Cairo, I understood better than ever before, that "Every language is its own river, with its own terrain and ecology, its own banks and tides, its own source and destinations where it empties, and therefore every writer who writes in that language must swim in its river." And every time I quoted him, my listener would silently agree, then I would too, and together we would share our appreciation for Mahfouz's words, and then I would admit that although they were hard to hear, they communicated a complicated truth, one for which I remain grateful. In all of my retellings, I have left out the bit about how after his sympathetic comment about Shakespeare, the conversation changed, in response to a question on realism and surrealism.

The truth is, that encounter with Mahfouz, like a dream, helped reveal something I already knew and toward which I was slowly, perhaps even unwillingly, making my way to, while missing it and resisting it. And as in all of our recounting of dreams and stories, we are involved in a creative act, selecting what to leave out and what to emphasize, and sometimes adding new bits. Obviously, much else happened during that evening in the hotel in Maadi, but our dreams and stories are ours not only because we are the best placed ones to tell and interpret them, but they are also there for our use, to make of them what we need. We reveal a great deal about ourselves through them. For beyond the social risk of boring others, our dreams and stories contain the most intimate details of our psyche. They are, whether we understand them or not, the temperament of our innermost self, the self that, at night or in our imagination, breaks free from the clasp of our conscious will.

It appears that, ever since his stabbing in 1994, the place and meaning of dreams changed for Mahfouz. They grew more vivid, or had come to seem more significant, because from then on, up until his death in 2006, he would write them down, capturing them in a few swift strokes. He did not only trust his subconscious, but trusted us with it. He published one volume under the title *Dreams During a Period of Convalescence*. The second volume came out posthumously under the title *The Last Dreams*. And it is that volume that has fascinated me most, not only because it contains some of Mahfouz's last writings, but also that translating them—I had no intention of doing so, but rather, one Sunday morning as I drank my coffee at the kitchen table, I thought of translating a couple for Diana and found, by the time she was up, I had done a dozen—felt like the most natural thing, as though I were stepping into their tide and all I had to do was let go, following their pull.

When I later mentioned this to my friend and Italian translator, Anna Nadotti, she said, "But that's how it is meant to be. Translation should be easy," and read me Giorgio Manganelli's words (in her translation): "If you translate a dream, it's impossible not to dream: but at the end the two dreams will be parallel, as those dreams that apparently lovers dream: similar and dissimilar, distant and tied by mutual intelligence and love."

These dreams are an insight into Mahfouz's twilight concerns. They are the dreams of an old man: regretful about missed opportunities, melancholy about the future. In the light of the present post–Tahrir Square Egypt, several of these dreams—dreamt about seven or more years before the Arab Spring—are oddly prophetic in how they depict national unrest and unfulfilled democratic yearnings. Asked what subject was closest to his heart, Mahfouz had replied, "Freedom. Freedom from colonization, freedom from the absolute rule of a king, and basic human freedom in the context of society and the family." Such aspirations are at play here: in the appearances of the founders of modern Egypt, men who yearned for freedom from British rule, chief among them Mahfouz's much-admired Saad Zaghloul; the freedom to love and live as one chooses; and, of course, Mahfouz's own personal desire to set his mind free from the bounds of consciousness.

They are also so personal in the way they contain his aptitude and appetite for the social life: friends and gatherings and, of course, his beloved city, Cairo. Almost each starts with "I saw myself" or "I found myself." And isn't that the case, that we find or see ourselves in dreams, believing in the promise that we're truly perceiving who we really are, and, in turn, are so deeply unsettled when we do not recognize ourselves in our dreams? There are many instances here, in Mahfouz's dreams, where we are unsure about the references or their meaning: we are very much inside a private world, written, perhaps, not for our eyes. And yet we cannot help detect in his dreams a pattern of repeated themes: the retention of hope in the worst of times; the failure of politics; the dream of democracy; love lost; mismatched yearnings. They are swift and brief, as though he were catching clouds or rescuing a fading image from oblivion, and the novelist's pen is visible, tempted to resolve or conclude the story. It is clear that Mahfouz, the professed realist, admired dreams, coveted their agile and wandering narratives, their convincing and often unsettling psychological and emotional power, and, perhaps most of all, their economy: how, in an instant, a world is evoked that is—no matter how unlikely or strange—convincingly compelling. The cumulative effect is a canvas of intimate communications, and yet, because Mahfouz has astutely refrained from any commentary or interpretation, the dreams are as formal as they are intimate. It is a contradiction that hums through them all.

At times we arrive with him at the shores of the morning, when, for example, he wakes up fatigued and confused from a dream of amorous dancing, or when he reads in the morning paper the obituary of his old lover B, of whom he had just been dreaming. B makes several appearances. She comes to embody both a painful longing as well as a hope, as though in approaching death he is coming nearer to her. It brings to mind Kamal, Abd al Jawad's youngest son in *The Cairo Trilogy*, the character Mahfouz admits is most like himself, who loves and loses Budur. And, of course, there is always Dante's Beatrice. As it is in Latin, the letter B in the Arabic alphabet comes second, and therefore suggests that the beloved is the companion-self, the partner and collaborator, the one who completes.

That same summer we met Naguib Mahfouz, when he was having some of the dreams contained in these pages, Cairo became Diana's muse. For the next several years she would go there and spend days and nights wandering the streets alone, photographing, until she came to know the city better than I do. Very much like an unforgettable dream, the images she captured are vivid, haunting, oddly mobile, uncertain. She kept them in a drawer for a long time. And as history moved on and it became, for political reasons, nearly impossible to photograph freely in the streets in Cairo, the images, like Mahfouz's dreams, began to seem the previsions of the diminished present. The distance between those we know best and their art is a curiously immeasurable one. These photographs are endlessly mysterious. They develop a conversation with Mahfouz's dreams that is suggestive and surprising. Both works are concerned with the same city-protagonist, Cairo, and both share a wandering and searching eye, often alighting on the most unlikely connections.

I like to imagine Mahfouz leafing through this book, with a treasured cigarette in one hand, discovering his own invisible lines between dream and image, and perhaps saying, in his soft and inimitable voice, "Of course."

I Found Myself . . .
The Last Dreams

Dream 200

I found myself preparing to confront a fierce enemy. My soul yearned for comfort and I climbed to the top floor. Looking down I saw the Great Muhammad Ali Pasha receiving the news and, as he listened, he grew in size until he lost his mind.

Dream 201

I saw myself walking to the house of my late friend A, to see if he wanted to join me at the café. He said he couldn't because today was his sister Zaynab's wedding. I went to the café without him and told everyone the news. They were all amazed, given how unattractive Zaynab was, and just then we saw the bride approach, followed by a procession of men and women all dressed in black, marching in orderly military fashion.

Dream 202

I found myself in a country cottage enveloped by silence and the night. The distant broken barks of my beautiful dog were the only sounds. Then gunshots. My friend went to inquire and after a short while returned to tell me, in a sad voice: They have killed your dog. Distressed, I began to cry. Were they thieves? I asked. He answered: Either that or else just troublemakers.

Dream 203

I found myself in a strange and sad place when suddenly there was my old love, B. She walked burdened by old age. Knowing that I will never see her again, I felt such deep sorrow.

Dream 204

I saw myself in my forties, caressing a pale rose. It responded, encouraging me, but, given our age difference, I hesitated. My reluctance persisted until she left, leaving me alone to contend with my aging self.

Dream 205

I saw myself studying law in order to please my father. For comfort, I secretly disappeared into song. And finally, when a choice had to be made, I became tormented. But my spirit won out in the end.

Dream 206

I found myself in a spacious and elegant hall. Gathered to one side were my family and friends and, at the opposite end, a door opened and through it my sweetheart B entered laughing, followed by her father. I lost all self-restraint and held my arms open wide. The imam began writing in the marriage book. Joy overtook everyone. My mother congratulated the bride and burned incense.

Dream 207

I found myself walking down a long road. A window of one of the houses to my left opened and through it appeared a woman's face. Although her beauty had disappeared behind a thick veil of ill health, and it had been fifty years since I had last seen her, I immediately recognized her. In the morning, I was deeply unsettled when, reading the newspaper, I came upon her obituary. I was profoundly saddened and wondered which of us had visited the other at that hour of death?

Dream 208

I found myself in my study. Mrs. S came to say goodbye before immigrating to another Arab county for work. She placed her hand in mine, and kept it there as her green eyes filled with tears.

Dream 209

I found myself sitting with President Jamal Abdel Nasser in a small garden, and he was saying: You may be asking why we don't meet as often anymore.

I said: I did wonder about that.

He said: It's because every time I consult you about an issue, I find that your opinion either partly or entirely contradicts mine, and so I feared for our friendship.

I replied: For me, our friendship—no matter our differences—can never end.

Dream 210

I found myself at Café El Fishawi. A short distance away was the famous artist and ballerina soon to announce her retirement. I couldn't help looking at her with great curiosity. She gracefully turned around and her lips gave me a faint smile. My companion said: Be glad, you won't embark on life's final battle alone.

Dream 211

I found myself facing a stage on which the leader Saad Zaghloul was sitting beside Mother Egypt. Suddenly a man approached, claiming to be the lady's true husband and asking her to follow him. He presented his papers, but the leader waved him away and said: We will let the law and the people decide.

Dream 212

I saw myself examining a picture the size of my palm: an etched portrait of a young man who looks like me and a young woman who resembles B. And, just then, I hear myself say: We have turned into a legend, one to be depicted and retold.

Dream 213

I found myself in the local wedding photographer's studio. Among the gallery of photographs, I spotted B. I examined her picture closely, taking my time, all the while enduring desperate regrets, and yet recognizing that I had not lost hope completely, and gleaning some solace from that fact.

Dream 214

I found myself at the tram stop, just as I realized that I had been pickpocketed. I then spotted my friend Ahmed, who appeared in a hurry. I rushed up to him and told him what had happened to me. He laughed, saying: I too was robbed. I said: Then let's go to El Abbassiya police station to find who took our money. He said, I urge you instead to volunteer for the new civil division, working directly with the Minister of the Interior, whose chief goal is to rid the country of pickpockets.

Dream 215

I saw myself among a group of young contemporaries. I noticed that one of them was neurotic and unstable. A young woman treated him with kind affection and he recovered his mental well-being. A deep love grew between them, but then his companions wanted to test him: They suggested I pretend to be the woman's lover. I did, and she politely rejected me. But then it was as if I truly loved her. It hurt that she preferred the other man who'd been unwell. Then, from far off, we heard coming the kind of music used to cure those possessed by demons. The woman began dancing. I went and danced with her until I woke up, exhausted on the shores of a new day.

Dream 216

I found myself in our old house in El Abbassiya, visiting my mother. She received me with perplexing indifference and then left the room. I assumed she'd gone to make coffee, but she never returned.

Dream 217

I found myself in a large demonstration that filled the squares and streets. Those in the front lines carried large photographs of Ahmed Urabi, Saad Zaghloul, and Mustafa al-Nahas. Their chants rang loudly, calling for a new constitution that was fit for the times. Unable to disperse the demonstrators, the security forces still appeared resolute.

Dream 218

I saw myself in a courtroom with some colleagues. I told the judge that I report to Technical Evaluations and have nothing to do with Oversight. He said my department fell under the responsibility of the director of Oversight and, therefore, it had nothing to do with Technical Evaluations. After our case was heard, the judge recommended that all technical committees include a representative from Oversight so that the Ministry will never again be obliged to issue ridiculous and contradictory decrees.

Dream 219

I saw myself as the head of a large family struggling to make ends meet. Eventually, my wife decided to help by making use of her excellent talent for cooking falafel. She found her first customers among our relatives, then the neighbors and, finally, our whole local district. "Glad tidings now that hardship has lifted."

Dream 220

I found myself at a police station, representing the residents of my street. Given the sharp increase in robberies, I asked the chief constable to assign a police officer to patrol our street at night. He said he has done that for another street and then when night fell the thieves had killed the officer. I asked if we could be permitted to carry arms to defend ourselves. He said that would make of us an even greater threat than the robbers. In that case, I asked, what do you suggest? He said: Keep the streetlights on and shut all your windows and doors.

Dream 221

I saw myself reading Saad Zaghloul's autobiography, taking great pleasure in its every detail, when suddenly I found the man himself sitting regally right in front of me. I rushed over and kissed his hand. I said: I have enjoyed every word in your book, but the printing is old and not befitting your stature. I asked his permission to publish a new edition. He granted it. I returned home to find that my wife had given birth to twins, a boy and a girl. We named the boy Saad and the girl Saada, and the days of ease returned and our hearts were gladdened.

Dream 222

I saw myself living through an era of great change, where all national borders were erased and—under the banner of justice, freedom, and the respect for human rights—all travel restrictions were lifted. I journeyed through the cities of the world and in each place found suitable employment, pleasurable distractions and excellent companions. Then I missed Egypt. I returned home and was greeted by my childhood friends. They asked me to tell them about my travels. I said: Let's first go to the old town and pray at Al Hussain Mosque, may God be content with him, and next have lunch at Al Dahan, then go on to Café El Fishawi to drink green tea and there I will tell you sheer wonders.

Dream 223

I saw my wife and myself struggling with a large suitcase when suddenly my old love B came to help us. I turned dizzy with joy. I touched her hand and said: I will never forget this for as long as I live. She replied: You must forget, for believe me I am happy with my husband and children. It was as though the very last candle had gone out.

Dream 224

I saw myself with her in the tea garden and she saying: You promised to visit my father and so my family have been expecting you. I told her that ever since I had discovered that I was twenty years her senior I'd grown reluctant, convinced that the marriage would be unfair to her. She said: But I don't mind. And I said: I don't want to be unjust or to abuse your innocence. Horrible, long, dark days passed before I learned that she'd married my colleague A. N. He and I were contemporaries and, what's more, he was a widower with a daughter old enough to get married herself. I remembered the poet who said:

He who listens to gossip will die of grief
While he who follows his desire is bold in his belief.

Dream 225

I found myself in my study, receiving a young woman. She was a distant relative of mine who'd come to tell me that her mother had passed away a week ago. I thought back on the beautiful old days that her mother and I had shared. Then the young woman said: Before my mother died, she told me that I should come to you if I ever needed advice. I told myself: God have mercy on her, she gave me a niece and now I must do all I can not to betray her trust in me.

Dream 226

I found myself with a battalion of soldiers in a trench covered with weeds. We waited for the right moment to surprise our enemy, while at the same time fearing that we might be discovered, that tear gas would be hurled into our bunker and we'd die the wretched death of rats.

Dream 227

I saw myself sitting with the late K on the balcony of his country house under the bright light of a full moon glowing in the deep heart of a rural night. He said: You know that I don't care much about politics, but despite that, the dawn patrol descended on me, blindfolded and dragged me to a dark cell where I spent a month without being charged or told the reason for my arrest. When I returned to my village, my nerves were shot, and that's how I met my end. I said: All the rabble walked in your funeral, speculating.

Dream 228

I found myself in Alexandria, walking into an elegant hotel and realizing that the manager was my beloved. I was overcome with joy and affection when she said: Why aren't we married yet? Remembering what happened between us in El Abbassiya, I said: I fear that if we get married, I might lose you. When I returned, I found that the hotel had closed down. The doorman told me the lady had returned to Athens, her hometown.

Dream 229

I found myself in Café Riche with my Café Riche friends. We were all waiting for the concert to begin. The members of the orchestra walked on: they were all there except for the maestro. My friends asked me to take his place and I managed the task successfully. The voices of Umm Kulthum and Abdel Wahhab permeated the café, along with those of the waiter and the owner. All the windows were opened and those outside joined the singing too, until music connected heaven and earth.

Dream 230

I saw myself in a pavilion that seemed to stretch into infinity. It was jam-packed with people. In the middle, one man preached about unity. When he was finished, I told him: Saad Zaghloul passed away, and so has Mustafa al-Nahas, so now our hopes for unity are pinned on you.

Dream 231

I saw Ibrahim Pasha emerge right out of his own statue and go wandering from café to café, challenging the top backgammon champions and defeating them one by one.

Dream 232

I found myself in the Al Ghouriya district and there were twice as many police as civilians. I saw my father walking toward me with a policeman on either side of him. I panicked, thinking he was under arrest. But then he greeted me and said: I see a policeman on either side of you, and I'm afraid you've been arrested.

Dream 233

I found myself in our old house in El Abbassiya, with my mother and sisters overcome with grief over the death of our faithful and much-loved dog. I had only ever seen them in such a state when the dearest to us had passed away.

Dream 234

I saw myself as the proprietor of a large farm around which I had built a modern village with clean running water and electricity. There was also a hospital, a school, a mosque, and a church. I'd doubled the wages of the workers. Then the warden of the district came to tell me: You stand accused of showing up the neighboring landlords and, therefore, of inciting anarchy and revolt among the innocent peasants.

Dream 235

I found myself in a group of young men listening to Osman Bouzi, the most prominent producer of perfumes during my youth: he was calling on us to boycott foreign goods. My father told me, sitting cross-legged on his prayer rug: That's all very well, but we haven't yet manufactured the most essential products. I told him: Well, let's start with what is possible.

Dream 236

I saw myself entering a new apartment, with the doorman leading the way. Then he was nowhere to be seen. I became homesick and wanted to leave, but I couldn't find my way out. Voices, offering guidance, began to direct me. Sometimes they said to turn right and other times left. I called out to the doorman, and then I called out to my family. Darkness fell, everything was confusion. And yet, somehow, I never altogether lost hope.

Dream 237

I saw myself entering the Garden of the Immortals in the El Gamaleya district. I was an adolescent again. I had on a pair of shorts. I saw a group of beautiful girls approach. They were about my age, led by the immortal Miss A. She smiled and my tears flowed till all her beauty vanished behind them.

Dream 238

I saw myself receiving a precious gift from the hand of the artist who was also a spiritual sheikh, and he was saying: You cannot enjoy it till you reach the place where the Nile meets the sea. I went there and found him waiting for me. We enjoyed the gift together. Our throats rang with sweet melodies until the blessed dawn call-to-prayer swam across the early moist air.

Dream 239

I found myself in a dense crowd. It was the day of global elections: all the nations participated and I saw kings, presidents, and the elite disguised as peasant girls. They sang the most noble and beautiful songs. I cast my vote and wondered: What will the results be tomorrow, what will their impact be on the country and on the nations of the world? All the polls predicted catastrophe.

Dream 240

I saw myself reading in my room. Outside, shouts came, slogans in various tongues. I closed the windows and drew the curtains, but then my friends stormed in, saying: We won't leave until you come with us—the time for solitude has passed.

Dream 241

After a long absence, I was invited to the national broadcasting building to discuss the question of abortion. A woman interviewer from the old days was my interlocutor. We exchanged warm greetings and I said: A coincidence is better than a thousand appointments—perhaps we'll make good use of it this time? She smiled and said: Perhaps we will.

Dream 242

Wherever I went, my lover's moon-bright face appeared: at work, at the places I frequented for amusement or pleasure, and again at the end of the day when I returned home to rest. At dawn she was there too, and I listened to her tender voice sound the praises of the Divine.

Dream 243

I found myself searching for evidence that my love was not an illusion but real. My lover had departed in the glory of her youth, and by now the witnesses too were gone. The features of our street had changed, and in the place of her house with its flower garden a high-rise block stood, densely populated. Nothing remained of the past except memories without proof.

Dream 244

I saw myself in the office, standing with my colleagues in front of the general manager. He looked at us with disappointment, and asked: How could you sell the chairs you used to sit on? One of the more senior individuals among us replied: We'd rather stand than starve to death.

Dream 245

I found myself in the middle of a large crowd gathered to witness the state visit of the Emperor of Japan. At the same time, the prime minister, Mustafa al-Nahas, was leaving a dentist's office: we followed him with our hearts and eyes until he disappeared inside his car. I thought, how odd it was that the two men, and for completely different reasons, shared the same tragedy.

Dream 246

I saw myself visiting Mrs. M to check on her health. I was close to her children, familiar with the differences that divided them. Each one blamed the other for having caused the kind lady's illness, so I told them: If you don't resolve your disputes immediately, you might kill her.

Dream 247

I found myself with some of my old Abbassia neighborhood friends, preparing to join the festivities for the Prophet's birthday: on our way there, we passed my beloved's house and, as we did, a secret ecstasy filled me. In the square, we toured the pavilions and listened to the Sufi chants. At midnight, the fireworks shot up and exploded, filling the night sky with pearls of light in various vivid shapes, illuminating the dome of the heavens. On my way home, back along the same route, I was once more captured by that ecstasy.

Dream 248

I saw myself among the crowds visiting the annual Agricultural Industry Fair. I passed by the various stalls when suddenly Prime Minister Mustafa al-Nahas appeared. The crowd rushed toward him, chanting his name. Security forces stormed the fair, beating everyone back with sticks. A few shots were fired. Two students died, one of whom was the son of the head of the security forces, and that became the talk of the town.

Dream 249

I found myself with my family in our Abbassia home, climbing up through all the rooms until we reached the roof. There we found several jars, each containing a dead scorpion half-submerged in an oily liquid. My mother said: Here's the cure if you get stung by a scorpion. I looked over the fence behind me and saw, stretching ahead and to the left, endless green pastures. On the right, there was a forest of prickly pears and, in the street parallel to it, houses ran in a row. Among them, there was the home where I would later witness days of joy and days of sorrow.

Dream 250

The production, distribution, and consumption of peanuts spread across the land and the industry formed a powerful lobby. The government could bear it no longer and issued a law prohibiting peanuts. The reaction was severe. Crowds of demonstrators filled the streets and the security forces failed to disperse them. The regime fell and completely disintegrated. The peanut industry flourished, cultivating new varieties that dominated the international market. Money poured in and a new era began in which political and economic difficulties—issues of unemployment, education and healthcare—were dealt with honestly and effectively. This was deemed a revolution and later was to be referred to as the Blessed Peanut Revolt.

Dream 251

I found myself leading a band and I invited the members to rehearse in my apartment, which was on the ground floor of a villa in the Bein Al Janayen district. An exceptionally beautiful woman knocked on the door. She said she lived upstairs and couldn't sleep from the noise. This is how we earn our living, I told her. She recommended we go speak to the chief constable. The police station was located in a square where three roads met and it was planted with fruit trees. A heavenly stillness hovered over the place. We presented the matter to the chief constable and he said the solution was to have my band rehearse in the station instead and he invited the lady to attend. I told him: I fear this will hinder your work. He said: Two years have passed now without a single violation or dispute. I brought the band and we sang "The beauty of your garden is your goodness." The lady rejoiced and sang with us, and her voice was as beautiful as her face.

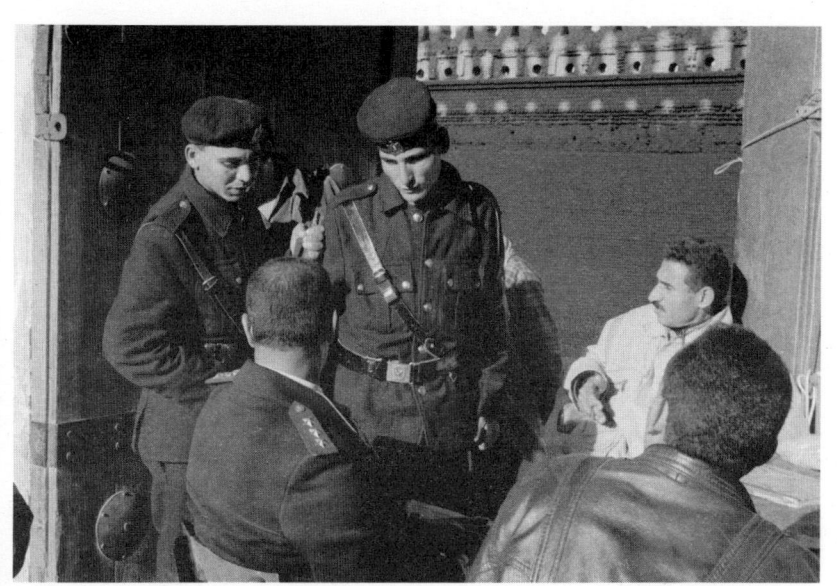

Dream 252

I saw myself among an audience listening to Professor A's lecture. A man stood up and objected, claiming that the professor was violating sacred rules, and he wouldn't stop complaining. The professor considered this an attack on his freedom of speech and stormed off the stage. An argument ensued. The head of the symposium urged everyone to debate calmly and to resort to reason, but tensions intensified and we were warned of violent clashes.

Dream 253

It was a day dedicated to celebrating the memory of Abbas Mahmoud al-Aqqad. A crowd flocked to the ballroom. There I met Doctor A, whom I hadn't seen for ages. She was to present her research on al-Aqqad's prose style and I on his poetry. I was reminded of our younger days, when she and I were brought together by dreams, dreams that never came true. I asked her to meet me right after our lectures. She smiled and, although she did not say a word, I understood that she'd consented.

Dream 254

My sister's son got his law degree and wanted to go spend a week in Alexandria. He set off in the morning, but by noon I found him standing in front of me. I asked him what had brought him back. He said: The truth is that death caught up with me while I was looking for a vacant room, so I returned to bid you farewell. I said goodbye with abundant tears in my eyes.

Dream 255

I found myself sinking deeper into the streets of the popular neighborhood until I reached a cart selling lupines. A woman stood by, leaning her arm on it. I recognized her, but only with some difficulty. She approached, asking how I had managed to find her. I told her: A friend from the old days, who'd told me the whole story, gave me directions. Then with great emotion she said: I lost everything and was denied the world. I have nothing left with which to secure a living except for this cart. I told her that I would not abandon her, and she replied, her eyes filling with tears: And I promise you true repentance.

Dream 256

I have never forgotten the story of my friend H, whose father set him up with a bookshop on one of the main avenues and supplied him with the best books with which to start his professional career. H employed a beautiful girl to help him. Years passed and the girl became the owner of the bookshop and she hired H as her assistant.

Dream 257

I saw myself observing a European setting up a barbershop next door to the old barber where, since childhood, we all went to get our hair cut. When he opened, he announced that his establishment would be for women only. I said: The European is ignorant of our traditions and will soon go bust. But a brave bride went to him, and her beautiful hairstyle became the best advertisement and soon the European was a huge success with brides—ordinary women as well as high society ladies. Then the European offered an irresistible sum to buy out our old barber. The European succeeded and was now serving both men and women, with no competitors to challenge him.

Dream 258

I found my father losing his temper at my mother and throwing her out of the house. I was madly angry at him and demanded: How dare you kick her out of her own house? He slapped me across the face. My outburst turned more severe. He, fearful of scandal and of what the neighbors might say, told me: Go now and get your mother. But I screamed in his face: Go and get her yourself. My father went to my grandmother's house and my mother returned home, her honor and dignity restored.

Dream 259

The husband of my darling B had gone away to a science conference and I invited her to meet me. We were walking in Hadaeq Al Qubbah, when we saw someone approach from a distance. My beloved trembled and said: That man is a judge and a friend of my husband. We agreed to go to Alexandria, to be away from prying eyes, but just as the train was pulling into the station, we saw standing on the platform, as though waiting for us, the judge. Fearing the consequences, we decided to abandon our plans and go our separate ways.

Dream 260

I found myself listening to her as she said: It was your kindness that cured me of a fatal disease. I told her: I too am in need of kindness. She said: Very well, but you are sixteen and I am in my fifties. To which I then said: A year full of kindness is better than a lifetime without.

Dream 261

I saw myself looking at the late S as he told me: I came to apologize because I loved having children but have now left you with the heavy burden of caring for them. I said to him: Your intentions were good, and no one could have expected your premature death. I remember you walking to the noble Al Hussein's mosque for the dawn prayer.

Dream 262

I found my uncle and his wife sitting in front of my father and saying: We want your son for our daughter. He told them: But it'll be a while still before he can afford to get married. They said: Blessing be upon you who can help him, just as you have his brothers. My father replied: But we are in a crisis now and I am suffering. They left disappointed. When my father died, my uncle came crying, which made me wonder: Were his tears of grief or of remorse?

Dream 263

I saw myself sitting with my cousin and she was telling me: There is no shame in a mother choosing the right husband for her daughter. I said: But you know our circumstances. She said: You won't have to pay a single penny. I said: But this is exactly what I cannot accept.

Dream 264

I found myself in Alexandria, spending a month's vacation. I opened the windows of the seaside cabin and breathed in the beautiful air. A European girl passed by and asked if she could change her clothes in my cabin. I said she could and there began a friendship that lasted the whole month. When our happy time together ended and we were about to go our separate ways, I sat down and wrote her a farewell letter. Then I headed to my car and there, sitting inside, I found her waiting for me. She smiled and said: What kept you so long?

Dream 265

I found myself standing on a busy station platform. The train had two sections: one for common folk, which was crowded and filled with the aroma of traditional foods, and the other was extremely clean and elegant. I said to my friend: The first section doesn't have an atmosphere conducive for our work. My friend replied: Yes, but I spotted some of our opponents in the other section. I said: I am ready for a confrontation.

Dream 266

I found myself at the aquarium and my friend was telling me: She is willing to return and is full of good promises. I said: I no longer trust her or her promises. He said: One must, for as long as we are alive, retain some good faith.

Dream 267

The drums of joy beat in the old house. My family gathered and, because I was unmarried and childless, they praised me for living carefree and unburdened. They asked me to demonstrate some of my clowning tricks, so I danced and I amazed them. Then I made them sing songs that are only heard in bad, scandalous establishments. When the evening concluded, I found myself alone with the night, heading to my empty house.

Dream 268

I found myself among a group of friends declaring their intentions to emigrate abroad. They urged me to join them, but I, of course, declined. But there was another group that traveled annually, only for the purposes of observation and reflection, each time returning more knowledgeable and more able to be of good use to others, so I joined them.

Dream 269

I was invited by the late engineer D to observe one of his new inventions. I sat with the others while the deceased informed us that he had designed a new engine, one which he had already successfully tested. He sat behind the steering wheel of the small car and pressed a button: a fire engulfed the vehicle and him with it. The smell of death remains in my nostrils.

Dream 270

I saw myself returning from work to our house in Abbassiya. I stood for a time by the window, looking out at the house where my beloved had lived in the years before she married. Then my sister came to tell me: She died giving birth to her second child. I turned rigid and felt as though the world had lost its light.

Dream 271

I saw myself as a soccer star playing on the national team. Despite my young age and slight build, my dribbling and scoring skills quickly attracted attention. Fans of the opposing team began urging their players to tackle me. I was surrounded, then the ball took me and carried me up: all were astonished, their eyes following me upwards. The ball kept rising until I disappeared with it into the clouds.

Dream 272

I found myself holding Aladdin's lamp. I asked the genie to bring my beloved A. back from the dead. And just then I was back to being a minor employee, a writer who failed to have his work published anywhere, watching a demonstration and listening to the frightening chant: "Rommel, advance." I saw Nazi and fascist banners waving in the air and a dark despair spread across millions of people. My beloved rushed to the lamp and begged the genie to return things to how they were before.

Dream 273

I found myself in a room underground. A man approached. At first, what with his shabby clothes and sad face, I took him for a beggar, but then I recognized him and ran over to greet him warmly. He teared up and told me that I was the only one among all of his colleagues who didn't ignore him or wasn't disgusted by him. I asked him to tell me his story. He said that someone envious had framed him. He'd been accused of smoking hashish and sentenced to a year in prison. There he was damaged and tormented, and gradually he lost all sense of the past and the future. I asked him whatever became of our fellow colleague whom he had intended to marry. He said she'd snubbed him and that he didn't blame her. How could she be expected to present her father with a groom who was a drug addict with a criminal record?! I said: But no one can dismiss your talents. He said: Forget all that and allow me to leave before anyone sees us together and suspects you too.

Dream 274

I saw myself in the Orman Botanical Gardens, surrounded by memories as vivid as the trees. We listened to songs and poetry, exchanged shy looks with our female colleagues, and pretended to cry out for freedom, sensing that the grass beneath us had once been soaked in the blood of martyrs.

Dream 275

I found myself kissing her. We were older and had overcome our shyness. She told me that in her younger years she had wished to marry me, and that she had tried to give off all the right signs but I, as though in a stupor, hadn't noticed. I remembered that stupor of first love, which had struck me back then with its heavenly delights and gloomy sorrows.

Dream 276

I was invited to join the admissions committee of a girls' music academy. Wanting to be comfortable, I went dressed in a simple robe rather than a suit and tie. My fiancée, who was the academy's head teacher, frowned when she saw me. She said: One ought to make a good impression on the students or else they'll think that this is not a place for serious learning but for play. She then whispered in the ear of one of the committee members that she wished to teach me the correct modes of conduct. My heart sank, and, long after, this was the forgotten reason behind my breaking off our engagement.

Dream 277

I found myself with a friend in a garden. He said: Doubtless you loved her. I said: I did then, and I still do. He said: So why did you back out at the very last minute? I said: She did not restrain her affections, and I became completely gripped by an inexplicable panic that drove me away in torment.

Dream 278

I found myself falling in love with a girl who was parading her graceful figure and waving to me from a balcony. We signaled to meet at the tram station. But when we did, I was surprised to find that she was different from what I had imagined. It seemed the disappointment was mutual—she never again appeared on the balcony.

Dream 279

By a fortunate turn of events, I was offered a spot on the national soccer team. At the same time, I was given an award and had to travel abroad in order to receive it. I struggled with what to do, but then my neighbor—hearing about my engagement, which was yet to be formally announced—offered to travel in my place, and that was how she and I began a prosperous and playful life together.

Dream 280

I found myself in a garden covered with flowers, but which had just one mature tree. I asked the gardener: Why is this the only tree in the entire garden? He said: Because its beauty is unmatched, its grace has no equal, its admirers are countless and so are its victims. Who would dare to try to match it?

Dream 281

During the Prophet's birthday festivities, I found myself moving among the confectionery stalls. One of the shopkeepers said: Have some of this white candy, as it will steady your heart, and take some of the red ones—with these the gates of heaven open and a person flies without wings.

Dream 282

I found myself reading in my room. In the next room, my late mother was sitting cross-legged on the prayer rug, and my attractive relative, the likewise deceased A, was dancing naked and singing a moving song. My mother was annoyed and told her: Don't distract him from his work.

Dream 283

I found myself at an international fair, standing in front of the honey section. I asked the salesman about a brand that had been widely advertised in newspapers and on foreign television channels. He said it was indeed available, but rather expensive and that some people found it hard on the stomach. I bought it, determined that I'd be among those who would easily digest it.

Dream 284

I found myself restored to a state of pure love, praying at its temple. But then, driven by feverish desires, I began to have secret encounters with young ladies, and no sooner was my lust quenched than I was left heavy with self-disgust and deep remorse. To purify myself, I bathed and prayed, and then returned to the temple.

Dream 285

I saw in my sleep that I owned a piece of land. A dispute arose over it. I resorted to the courts and they ruled that I was the sole owner. But my adversaries did not respect the ruling. The dispute continued and I began to receive threats. And one night, as I walked home, I was assaulted. The case became widely known and I refused to give up my legitimate rights.

Dream 286

I saw myself taking part in a silent demonstration that had filled the streets and squares. I noticed among the faces people who, at one point or another, had departed from this world. They broke the silence and turned the demonstration into a loud and hostile one. The atmosphere became tensed and charged with danger.

Dream 287

I found myself in a train carriage among the rabble as Doctor S preached about the different types of love. She said: And now I will tell you how best to choose a suitable kind of love. Just then our carriage broke off from the rest of the train, separating us from the doctor, and we tumbled across the desert without direction.

Dream 288

I saw myself sitting with some intellectuals at the house of the journalist M. He was telling us about the different types of torment that have afflicted him—in childhood, adolescence, youth, and old age—and then he said: There is another misery that haunts me from time to time. I do not know the reason for it. I have invited you here today to help me reveal its nature. And just as he finished saying this, his soul left him. We became so occupied with his death that we could scarcely think of anything else.

Dream 289

I found myself in a pavilion that stretched to an exceptional length and breadth, headed by the leader Saad Zaghloul. He had gathered the delegates there: the living among them and the dead, those who had been struck off the Wafd Party as well as the pashas from the Free Constitutionalists Party, the Independents, and those from other political parties. Saad said that he had asked to meet the chief official, and that he would go to him, accompanied by Shaarawi Pasha, Abdel Aziz Fahmi, and Mustafa Al Nahhas, in order to present the demands of the nation. The attendees stood up and applauded.

Dream 290

There was a well-off man who was married to two beautiful women. He went home at the end of the day and found them well and the coals burning in the fireplace, the hashish pipe cleaned thoroughly inside and out, and the dinner all set. The waterpipe turned and all three of their heads turned, and the two wives talked about what they had heard in the market. The man said: The world is well and dear old Egypt is well—only the envious would say otherwise. Dinner was served, made up of meat, falafel, cheese, and beans, while the main dish was the basbousa.

Dream 291

I saw myself with my late friend, the barrister A, and with us was an official from the ministry assigned to determine A's inheritance from his mother's estate. I had a young lady with me and introduced her to my friend as my fiancée. He was surprised and said: But no one told me that you got engaged. I replied: We have postponed announcing it until the war ends and my brother returns safely.

Dream 292

I found myself at an exhibition by the artist S, standing in front of a portrait of A, my adored love. I told the artist: You altered her facial features. He said: One of the characteristics of true art is that it is not bound by reality. I replied: But I wish you had remained true to the original for she is an ideal that requires no alteration. I remained standing in front of the picture, my eyes fixed on it.

Dream 293

I saw myself playing on Egypt's national soccer team, taking part in some of the most important matches of the year. Among the spectators, I glimpsed A, sitting beside her husband. I played my best and the crowd cheered and called out my name, which, for a little while, gladdened my sad heart.

Dream 294

I found myself standing in front of the tax inspector, presenting to him my annual accounts. He examined them with a stern face, writing down the taxes due. I was then sent to an underground chamber that housed the Office of the Budget. It was filled with safes and employees. I paid the required taxes to one of the officials and he began counting the money. I then noticed that instead of fingers he had claws. I trembled and he said: We know that we are not loved, but we collect money for the state to spend on national development projects. I said: But where are those projects? He pointed to a door. When I passed through it, strong men shook my hand but then threw me to the ground, and proceeded to beat me with sticks.

Dream 295

Early in the morning, I was getting ready to leave the hotel when I discovered that I had lost my watch. I thought of calling the police, but when I got to the lobby, I found my darling B standing there. I wondered what had brought her? I had not seen her since her wedding. We had a brief conversation and then she left. I looked at the parrot in the cage that was hanging from the ceiling and told him: You are the one who knows everything about my lost watch. The parrot replied: I still love you, you so-and-so. My heart quickened as that was the exact sentence that I had said to B. I gave up on the watch, packed my bag and left the hotel, with the parrot's voice chasing me out, repeating: I still love you, you so-and-so.

Dream 296

Outside my friend T's house, I found his servant bleeding. He said: See how your friend treats me? And all this just because I was a minute late with his tea. The servant departed and inside I found my friend in one of his fits of rage, threatening to shoot me. I ran out and found the servant's family. They said: Your friend is acting as though we live in a lawless land. They burst in on him and he opened fire. They pummeled him with stones from all directions until he fell unconscious.

Dream 297

I saw myself sitting in a café eating my dinner. Nearby sat a lady of the night, eyeing my food. I waved to her to join me and, without a moment's hesitation, she accepted and proceeded to greedily attack my plate. I lost my appetite and got up to leave when she objected, saying: If you do not stay with me, this would be considered charity and I firmly refuse to be mistaken for a beggar.

Dream 298

I found myself walking in the dark, with a ghost moving about me. I was terrified. I took refuge by the statue of Saad Zaghloul. The leader jumped off the pedestal to the ground and woke up the lion that was beside him. It started roaring. And suddenly, the ghost vanished and peace returned to my heart. I thanked the honorable leader and walked across the bridge in peace.

Dream 299

I saw myself on a visit to Japan. A guide led me from one unique monument to another, telling me: Many would not have imagined that Japan would be suitable for freedom and democracy, and yet here it is at the forefront of free nations. And I sensed, after all my pessimism, hope returning.